CARTOON NETWORK™ SCOOBY-DOO!™ PICTURE CLUE BOOK

THE SCARECROW MYSTERY

By Shannon Penney • Illustrated by Duendes del Sur

Hello Reader — Level 1

WORLDWIDE PUBLISHING™

SCHOLASTIC INC.

New York   Toronto   London   Auckland   Sydney
Mexico City   New Delhi   Hong Kong   Buenos Aires

ISBN 0-439-78548-0

12   11   10   9   8   7   6   5   4   3   2   6   7   8   9   10/0

Designed by Michael Massen
Printed in the U.S.A.
First printing, October 2005

and were visiting a patch with their friends. They each picked a big from the field. couldn't wait to put a inside his and make a funny .

The gang carried their 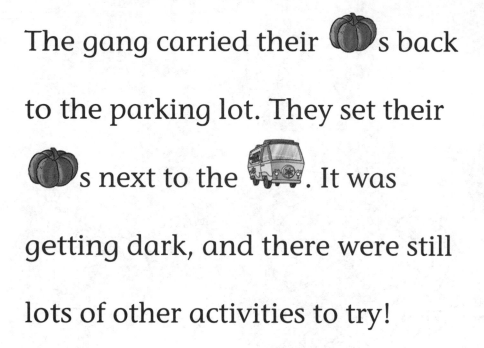s back to the parking lot. They set their s next to the . It was getting dark, and there were still lots of other activities to try!

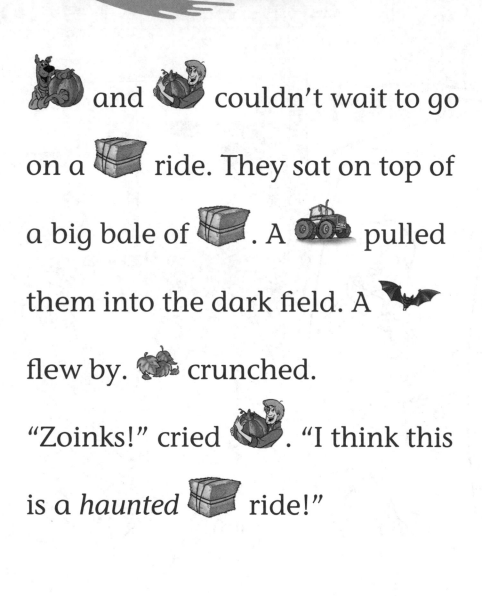 and couldn't wait to go on a ride. They sat on top of a big bale of . A pulled them into the dark field. A flew by. crunched.

"Zoinks!" cried . "I think this is a *haunted* ride!"

Just then,  spotted a spooky right behind . The wore a big, floppy .

"Ruh-roh!" cried, pointing. turned around. "RUN!" he yelled. They jumped off the ride and ran back to the .

and were out of breath

when they got to the .

They'd escaped the spooky .

But something wasn't quite right.

"Hey, !" said . "Our

s are missing! What if the

took them?"

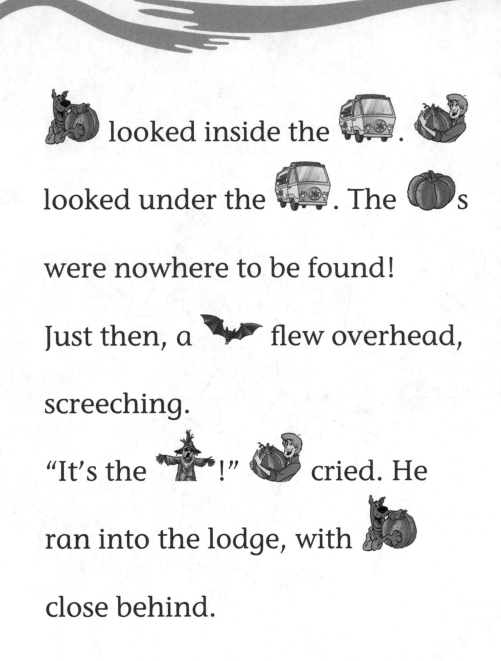

looked inside the . looked under the . The s were nowhere to be found! Just then, a flew overhead, screeching.

"It's the !" cried. He ran into the lodge, with close behind.

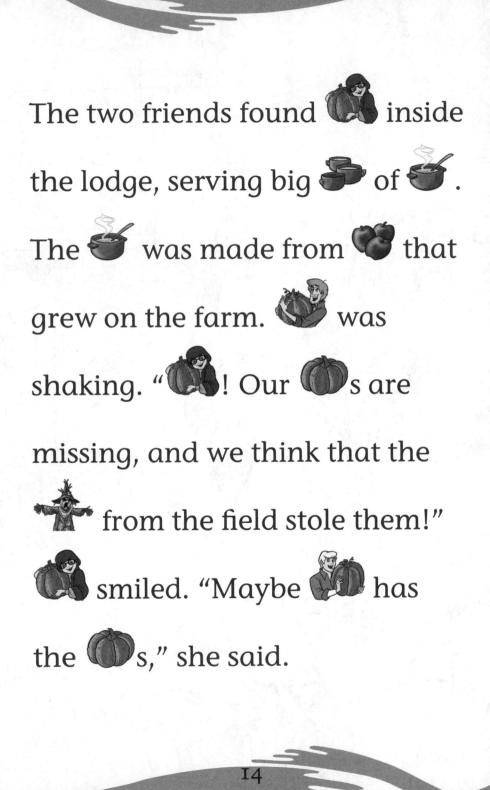

The two friends found ![] inside the lodge, serving big ![] of ![]. The ![] was made from ![] that grew on the farm. ![] was shaking. "![]! Our ![]s are missing, and we think that the ![] from the field stole them!" ![] smiled. "Maybe ![] has the ![]s," she said.

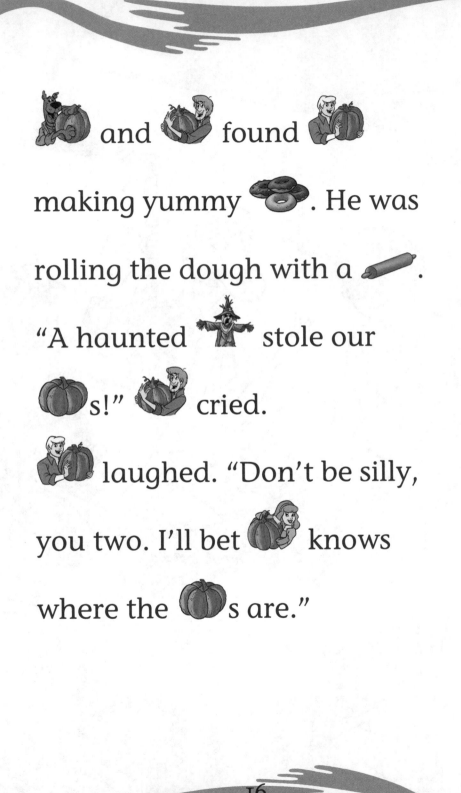

and found

making yummy . He was

rolling the dough with a .

"A haunted stole our

s!" cried.

laughed. "Don't be silly,

you two. I'll bet knows

where the s are."

"Let's go, !" called,

running through the lodge.

 was in the kitchen,

sprinkling with . She was

going to roast them in the .

When they reached her,

was out of breath. "Our s

were stolen by an evil !" he

said.

laughed. "An evil 🎃?" she asked.

"Rup!" 🐕🎃 said. He was so scared, his teeth were nearly chattering!

Just then, the 📟 timer went off. 👧🎃 opened the 📟 and pulled out five 🍪!

 and walked into the

kitchen. "Surprise!" they yelled.

" used the insides of the s

to make for you!"

"And I saved the outsides of the

s so you could carve s,"

 said.

 was so excited, he took a big

bite of right then and there.

"Scooby-dooby-doo!" he cheered.

Did you spot all the picture clues in this Scooby-Doo mystery?

Each picture clue is on a flash card. Ask a grown-up to cut out the flash cards. Then try reading the words on the back of the cards. The pictures will be your clue.

Reading is fun with Scooby-Doo!

Shaggy	Scooby
Fred	Daphne
Velma	pumpkin

candle	jack-o'-lantern
Mystery Machine	tractor
hay	bat

leaves

scarecrow

hat

cider

mugs

apples

doughnuts	rolling pin
pumpkin seeds	salt
pumpkin pies	oven